Shipping Clerk

Joseph Samachson

Alpha Editions

This edition published in 2023

ISBN : 9789357941785

Design and Setting By
Alpha Editions
www.alphaedis.com
Email - info@alphaedis.com

Shipping Clerk
By WILLIAM MORRISON

*If Ollie knew the work he was doing, he would
have resigned—if resigning were possible!*

If there had ever been a time when Ollie Keith hadn't been hungry, it
was so far in the past that he couldn't remember it. He was hungry
now as he walked through the alley, his eyes shifting lusterlessly from
one heap of rubbish to the next. He was hungry through and
through, all one hundred and forty pounds of him, the flesh
distributed so gauntly over his tall frame that in spots it seemed
about to wear through, as his clothes had. That it hadn't done so in
forty-two years sometimes struck Ollie as in the nature of a miracle.

He worked for a junk collector and he was unsuccessful in his
present job, as he had been at everything else. Ollie had followed the
first part of the rags-to-riches formula with classic exactness. He had
been born to rags, and then, as if that hadn't been enough, his
parents had died, and he had been left an orphan. He should have
gone to the big city, found a job in the rich merchant's counting
house, and saved the pretty daughter, acquiring her and her fortune
in the process.

It hadn't worked out that way. In the orphanage where he had spent
so many unhappy years, both his food and his education had been
skimped. He had later been hired out to a farmer, but he hadn't been
strong enough for farm labor, and he had been sent back.

His life since then had followed an unhappy pattern. Lacking
strength and skill, he had been unable to find and hold a good job.
Without a good job, he had been unable to pay for the food and
medical care, and for the training he would have needed to acquire
strength and skill. Once, in the search for food and training, he had
offered himself to the Army, but the doctors who examined him had
quickly turned thumbs down, and the Army had rejected him with
contempt. They wanted better human material than that.

How he had managed to survive at all to the present was another miracle. By this time, of course, he knew, as the radio comic put it, that he wasn't long for this world. And to make the passage to another world even easier, he had taken to drink. Rot gut stilled the pangs of hunger even more effectively than inadequate food did. And it gave him the first moments of happiness, spurious though they were, that he could remember.

Now, as he sought through the heaps of rubbish for usable rags or redeemable milk bottles, his eyes lighted on something unexpected. Right at the edge of the curb lay a small nut, species indeterminate. If he had his usual luck, it would turn out to be withered inside, but at least he could hope for the best.

He picked up the nut, banged it futilely against the ground, and then looked around for a rock with which to crack it. None was in sight. Rather fearfully, he put it in his mouth and tried to crack it between his teeth. His teeth were in as poor condition as the rest of him, and the chances were that they would crack before the nut did.

The nut slipped and Ollie gurgled, threw his hands into the air and almost choked. Then he got it out of his windpipe and, a second later, breathed easily. The nut was in his stomach, still uncracked. And Ollie, it seemed to him, was hungrier than ever.

The alley was a failure. His life had been a progression from rags to rags, and these last rags were inferior to the first. There were no milk bottles, there was no junk worth salvaging.

At the end of the alley was a barber shop, and here Ollie had a great and unexpected stroke of luck. He found a bottle. The bottle was no container for milk and it wasn't empty. It was standing on a small table near an open window in the rear of the barber shop. Ollie found that he could get it by simply stretching out his long, gaunt arm for it, without climbing in through the window at all.

He took a long swig, and then another. The liquor tasted far better than anything he had ever bought.

When he returned the bottle to its place, it was empty.

Strangely enough, despite its excellent quality, or perhaps, he thought, *because* of it, the whiskey failed to have its usual effect on him. It left him completely sober and clear-eyed, but hungrier than ever.

In his desperation, Ollie did something that he seldom dared to do. He went into a restaurant, not too good a restaurant or he would never have been allowed to take a seat, and ordered a meal he couldn't pay for.

He knew what would happen, of course, after he had eaten. He would put on an act about having lost his money, but that wouldn't fool the manager for more than one second. If the man was feeling good and needed help, he'd let Ollie work the price out washing dishes. If he was a little grumpy and had all the dishwashers he needed, he'd have them boot the tar out of Ollie and then turn him over to the police.

The soup was thick and tasty, although tasty in a way that no gourmet would have appreciated. The mess was food, however, and Ollie gulped it down gratefully. But it did nothing to satisfy his hunger. Likewise, the stew had every possible leftover thrown into it, and none of it gave Ollie any feeling of satisfaction. Even the dessert and the muddy coffee left him as empty as before.

The waiter had been in the back room with the cook. Now Ollie saw him signal to the manager, and watched the manager hasten back. He closed his eyes. They were onto him; there was no doubt about it. For a moment he considered trying to get out of the front door before they closed in, but there was another waiter present, keeping an eye on the patrons, and he knew that he would never make it. He took a deep breath and waited for the roof to fall in on him.

He heard the manager's foot-steps and opened his eyes. The manager said, "Uh—look, bud, about that meal you ate—"

"Not bad," observed Ollie brightly.

"Glad you liked it."

He noticed little beads of sweat on the manager's forehead, and wondered what had put them there. He said, "Only trouble is, it ain't fillin'. I'm just as hungry as I was before."

"It didn't fill you up, huh? That's too bad. I'll tell you what I'll do. Rather than see you go away dissatisfied, I won't charge you for the meal. Not a cent."

Ollie blinked. This made no sense whatever. All the same, if not for the gnawing in his stomach, he would have picked himself up and run. As it was, he said, "Thanks. Guess in that case I'll have another order of stew. Maybe this time it'll stick to my ribs."

"Not the stew," replied the manager nervously. "You had the last that was left. Try the roast beef."

"Hmm, that's more than I was gonna spend."

"No charge," said the manager. "For you, no charge at all."

"Then gimme a double order. I feel starved."

The double order went down the hatch, yet Ollie felt just as empty as ever. But he was afraid to press his luck too far, and after he had downed one more dessert—also without charge—he reluctantly picked himself up and walked out. He was too hungry to spend any more time wondering why he had got a free meal.

In the back room of the restaurant, the manager sank weakly into a chair. "I was afraid he was going to insist on paying for it. Then we'd really have been on a spot."

"Guess he was too glad to get it for free," the cook said.

"Well, if anything happens to him now, it'll happen away from here."

"Suppose they take a look at what's in his stomach."

"He still won't be able to sue us. What did you do with the rest of that stew?"

"It's in the garbage."

"Cover it up. We don't want dead cats and dogs all over the place. And next time you reach for the salt, make sure there isn't an insect powder label on it."

"It was an accident; it could happen to anybody," said the cook philosophically. "You know, maybe we shouldn't have let that guy go away. Maybe we ought to have sent him to a doctor."

"And pay his bills? Don't be a sap. From now on, he's on his own. Whatever happens to him, we don't know anything about it. We never saw him before."

The only thing that was happening to Ollie was that he was getting hungrier and hungrier. He had, in fact, never before been so ravenous. He felt as if he hadn't eaten in years.

He had met with two strokes of luck—the accessible bottle and the incredibly generous manager. They had left him just as hungry and thirsty as before. Now he encountered a third gift of fortune. On the plate glass window of a restaurant was the flamboyant announcement: eating contest tonight at monte's restaurant! For the Championship of the World! Entries Being Taken now! No Charge if you Eat Enough for at Least Three People.

Ollie's face brightened. The way he felt, he could have eaten enough for a hundred. The fact that the contestants, as he saw upon reading further, would be limited to hard-boiled eggs made no difference to him. For once he would have a chance to eat everything he could get down his yawning gullet.

That night it was clear that neither the judges nor the audience thought much of Ollie as an eater. Hungry he undoubtedly was, but it was obvious that his stomach had shrunk from years of disuse, and besides, he didn't have the build of a born eater. He was long and skinny, whereas the other contestants seemed almost as broad and wide as they were tall. In gaining weight, as in so many other things, the motto seemed to be that those who already had would get more. Ollie had too little to start with.

In order to keep the contest from developing an anticlimax, they started with Ollie, believing that he would be lucky if he ate ten eggs.

Ollie was so ravenous that he found it difficult to control himself, and he made a bad impression by gulping the first egg as fast as he could. A real eater would have let the egg slide down rapidly yet gently, without making an obvious effort. This uncontrolled, amateur speed, thought the judges, could only lead to a stomachache.

Ollie devoured the second egg, the third, the fourth, and the rest of his allotted ten. At that point, one of the judges asked, "How do you feel?"

"Hungry."

"Stomach hurt?"

"Only from hunger. It feels like it got nothin' in it. Somehow, them eggs don't fill me up."

Somebody in the audience laughed. The judges exchanged glances and ordered more eggs brought on. From the crowd of watchers, cries of encouragement came to Ollie. At this stage, there was still nobody who thought that he had a chance.

Ollie proceeded to go through twenty eggs, forty, sixty, a hundred. By that time, the judges and the crowd were in a state of unprecedented excitement.

Again a judge demanded, "How do you feel?"

"Still hungry. They don't fill me up at all."

"But those are large eggs. Do you know how much a hundred of them weigh? Over fifteen pounds!"

"I don't care how much they weigh. I'm still hungry."

"Do you mind if we weigh you?"

"So long as you don't stop givin' me eggs, okay."

They brought out a scale and Ollie stepped on it. He weighed one hundred and thirty-nine pounds, on the nose.

Then he started eating eggs again. At the end of his second hundred, they weighed him once more. Ollie weighed one hundred thirty-eight and three-quarters.

The judges stared at each other and then at Ollie. For a moment the entire audience sat in awed silence, as if watching a miracle. Then the mood of awe passed.

One of the judges said wisely, "He palms them and slips them to a confederate."

"Out here on the stage?" demanded another judge. "Where's his confederate? Besides, you can see for yourself that he eats them. You can watch them going down his throat."

"But that's impossible. If they really went down his throat, he'd gain weight."

"I don't know how he does it," admitted the other. "But he does."

"The man is a freak. Let's get some doctors over here."

Ollie ate another hundred and forty-three eggs, and then had to stop because the restaurant ran out of them. The other contestants never even had a chance to get started.

When the doctor came and they told him the story, his first impulse seemed to be to grin. He knew a practical joke when he heard one. But they put Ollie on the scales—by this time he weighed only a hundred thirty-eight and a quarter pounds—and fed him a two pound loaf of bread. Then they weighed him again.

He was an even one hundred and thirty-eight.

"At this rate, he'll starve to death," said the doctor, who opened his little black bag and proceeded to give Ollie a thorough examination.

Ollie was very unhappy about it because it interfered with his eating, and he felt more hungry than ever. But they promised to feed him afterward and, more or less unwillingly, he submitted.

"Bad teeth, enlarged heart, lesion on each lung, flat feet, hernia, displaced vertebrae—you name it and he has it," said the doctor. "Where the devil did he come from?"

Ollie was working on an order of roast beef and was too busy to reply.

Somebody said, "He's a rag-picker. I've seen him around."

"When did he start this eating spree?"

With stuffed mouth, Ollie mumbled, "Today."

"Today, eh? What happened today that makes you able to eat so much?"

"I just feel hungry."

"I can see that. Look, how about going over to the hospital so we can really examine you?"

"No, sir," said Ollie. "You ain't pokin' no needles into me."

"No needles," agreed the doctor hastily. If there was no other way to get blood samples, they could always drug him with morphine and he'd never know what had happened. "We'll just look at you. And we'll feed you all you can eat."

"All I can eat? It's a deal!"

The humor was crude, but it put the point across—the photographer assigned to the contest had snapped a picture of Ollie in the middle of gulping two eggs. One was traveling down his gullet, causing a lump in his throat, and the other was being stuffed into his mouth at the same time. The caption writer had entitled the shot: the man who broke the icebox at monte's, and the column alongside was headed, Eats Three Hundred and Forty-three Eggs. "I'm Hungry!" He Says.

Zolto put the paper down. "This is the one," he said to his wife. "There can be no doubt that this person has found it."

"I knew it was no longer in the alley," said Pojim. Ordinarily a comely female, she was now deep in thought, and succeeded in looking beautiful and pensive at the same time. "How are we to get it back without exciting unwelcome attention?"

"Frankly," said Zolto, "I don't know. But we'd better think of a way. He must have mistaken it for a nut and swallowed it. Undoubtedly the hospital attendants will take X-rays of him and discover it."

"They won't know what it is."

"They will operate to remove it, and then they will find out."

Pojim nodded. "What I don't understand," she said, "is why it had this effect. When we lost it, it was locked."

"He must have opened it by accident. Some of these creatures, I have noticed, have a habit of trying to crack nuts with their teeth. He must have bitten on the proper switch."

"The one for inanimate matter? I think, Zolto, that you're right. The stomach contents are collapsed and passed into our universe through the transfer. But the stomach itself, being part of a living creature, cannot pass through the same switch. And the poor creature continually loses weight because of metabolism. Especially, of course, when he eats."

"Poor creature, you call him? You're too soft-hearted, Pojim. What do you think we'll be if we don't get the transfer back?"

He hunched up his shoulders and laughed.

Pojim said, "Control yourself, Zolto. When you laugh, you don't look human, and you certainly don't sound it."

"What difference does it make? We're alone."

"You can never tell when we'll be overheard."

"Don't change the subject. What are we supposed to do about the transfer?"

"We'll think of a way," said Pojim, but he could see she was worried.

In the hospital, they had put Ollie into a bed. They had wanted a nurse to bathe him, but he had objected violently to this indignity, and finally they had sent in a male orderly to do the job. Now, bathed, shaven and wearing a silly little nightgown that made him ashamed to look at himself, he was lying in bed, slowly starving to death.

A dozen empty plates, the remains of assorted specialties of the hospital, filled with vitamins and other good things, lay around him. Everything had tasted fine while going down, but nothing seemed to have stuck to him.

All he could do was brood about the puzzled and anxious looks on the doctors' faces when they examined him.

The attack came without warning. One moment Ollie was lying there unhappily, suffering hunger pangs, and the next moment somebody had punched him in the stomach. The shock made him start and then look down. But there was nobody near him. The doctors had left him alone while they looked up articles in textbooks and argued with each other.

He felt another punch, and then another and another. He yelled in fright and pain.

After five minutes, a nurse looked in and asked casually, "Did you call?"

"My stomach!" groaned Ollie. "Somebody's hittin' me in my stomach!"

"It's a tummyache," she said with a cheerful smile. "It should teach you not to wolf your food."

Then she caught a glimpse of his stomach, from which Ollie, in his agony, had cast off the sheet, and she gulped. It was swollen like a watermelon—or, rather, like a watermelon with great warts. Lumps stuck out all over it.

She rushed out, calling, "Doctor Manson! Doctor Manson!"

When she returned with two doctors, Ollie was in such acute misery that he didn't even notice them. One doctor said, "Well, I'll be damned!" and began tapping the swollen stomach.

The other doctor demanded, "When did this happen?"

"Right now, I guess," replied the nurse. "Just a few minutes ago his stomach was as flat as the way it was when you saw it."

"We'd better give him a shot of morphine to put him out of his pain," said the first doctor, "and then we'll X-ray him."

Ollie was in a semi-coma as they lifted him off his bed and wheeled him into the X-ray room. He didn't hear a word of the ensuing discussion about the photographs, although the doctors talked freely in front of him—freely and profanely.

It was Dr. Manson who demanded, "What in God's name are those things, anyway?"

"They look like pineapples and grapefruit," replied the bewildered X-ray specialist.

"Square-edged pineapples? Grapefruit with one end pointed?"

"I didn't say that's what they are," returned the other defensively. "I said that's what they look like. The grapefruit could be eggplant," he added in confusion.

"Eggplant, my foot. How the devil did they get into his stomach, anyway? He's been eating like a pig, but even a pig couldn't have gotten those things down its throat."

"Wake him up and ask him."

"He doesn't know any more than we do," said the nurse. "He told me that it felt as if somebody was hitting him in the stomach. That's all he'd be able to tell us."

"He's got the damnedest stomach I ever heard of," marveled Dr. Manson. "Let's open it up and take a look at it from the inside."

"We'll have to get his consent," said the specialist nervously. "I know it would be interesting, but we can't cut into him unless he's willing."

"It would be for his own good. We'd get that unsliced fruit salad out of him." Dr. Manson stared at the X-ray plates again. "Pineapples, grapefruit, something that looks like a banana with a small bush on top. Assorted large round objects. And what looks like a nut. A small nut."

If Ollie had been aware, he might have told Dr. Manson that the nut was the kernel of the trouble. As it was, all he could do was groan.

"He's coming to," said the nurse.

"Good," asserted Dr. Manson. "Get a release, Nurse, and the minute he's capable of following directions, have him sign it."

In the corridor outside, two white-clad interns stopped at the door of Ollie's room and listened. They could not properly have been described as man and woman, but at any rate one was male and the other female. If you didn't look at them too closely, they seemed to be human, which, of course, was what they wanted you to think.

"Just as I said," observed Zolto. "They intend to operate. And their attention has already been drawn to the nut."

"We can stop them by violence, if necessary. But I abhor violence."

"I know, dear," Zolto said thoughtfully. "What has happened is clear enough. He kept sending all that food through, and our people analyzed it and discovered what it was. They must have been surprised to discover no message from us, but after a while they arrived at the conclusion that we needed some of our own food and they sent it to us. It's a good thing that they didn't send more of it at one time."

"The poor man must be in agony as it is."

"Never mind the poor man. Think of our own situation."

"But don't you see, Zolto? His digestive juices can't dissolve such unfamiliar chemical constituents, and his stomach must be greatly irritated."

She broke off for a moment as the nurse came past them, giving them only a casual glance. The X-ray specialist followed shortly, his face reflecting the bewilderment he felt as a result of studying the plate he was holding.

"That leaves only Dr. Manson with him," said Zolto. "Pojim, I have a plan. Do you have any of those pandigestive tablets with you?"

"I always carry them. I never know when in this world I'll run into something my stomach can't handle."

"Fine." Zolto stepped back from the doorway, cleared his throat, and began to yell, "Calling Dr. Manson! Dr. Manson, report to surgery!"

"You've been seeing too many of their movies," said Pojim.

But Zolto's trick worked. They heard Dr. Manson mutter, "Damn!" and saw him rush into the corridor. He passed them without even noticing that they were there.

"We have him to ourselves," said Zolto. "Quick, the tablets."

They stepped into the room, where Zolto passed a small inhalator back and forth under Ollie's nose. Ollie jerked away from it, and his eyes opened.

"Take this," said Pojim, with a persuasive smile. "It will ease your pain." And she put two tablets into Ollie's surprised mouth.

Automatically, Ollie swallowed and the tablets sped down to meet the collection in his stomach. Pojim gave him another smile, and then she and Zolto were out of the room.

To Ollie, things seemed to be happening in more and more bewildering fashion. No sooner had these strange doctors left than Dr. Manson came rushing back, cursing, in a way that would have shocked Hippocrates, the unknown idiot who had summoned him to surgery. Then the nurse came in, with a paper. Ollie gathered that he was being asked to sign something.

He shook his head vigorously. "Not me. I don't sign *nothin'*, sister."

"It's a matter of life and death. Your own life and death. We have to get those things out of your stomach."

"No, sir, you're not cuttin' me open."

Dr. Manson gritted his teeth in frustration. "You don't feel so much pain now because of the morphine I gave you. But it's going to wear off in a few minutes and then you'll be in agony again. You'll have to let us operate."

"No, sir," repeated Ollie stubbornly. "You're not cuttin' me open."

And then he almost leaped from his bed. His already distended stomach seemed to swell outward, and before the astonished eyes of doctor and nurse, a strange new bump appeared.

"Help!" yelled Ollie.

"That's exactly what we're trying to do," said Dr. Manson angrily. "Only you won't let us. Now sign that paper, man, and stop your nonsense."

Ollie groaned and signed. The next moment he was being rushed into the operating room.

The morphine was wearing off rapidly, and he lay, still groaning, on the table. From the ceiling, bright lights beat down upon him. Near his head the anesthetist stood with his cone of sleep poised in readiness. At one side a happy Dr. Manson was slipping rubber gloves on his antiseptic hands, while the attentive nurses and assistants waited.

Two interns were standing near the doorway. One of them, Zolto, said softly, "We may have to use violence after all. They must not find it."

"I should have given him a third tablet," said Pojim, the other intern, regretfully. "Who would have suspected that the action would be so slow?"

They fell silent. Zolto slipped a hand into his pocket and grasped the weapon, the one he had hoped he wouldn't have to use.

Dr. Manson nodded curtly and said, "Anesthetic."

And then, as the anesthetist bent forward, it happened. Ollie's uncovered stomach, lying there in wait for the knife, seemed to heave and boil. Ollie shrieked and, as the assembled medicos watched in dazed fascination, the knobs and bumps smoothed out. The whole stomach began to shrink, like a cake falling in when some one has slammed the oven door. The pandigestive tablets had finally acted.

Ollie sat up. He forgot that he was wearing the skimpy and shameless nightgown, forgot, too, that he had a roomful of spectators. He pushed away the anesthetist who tried to stop him.

"I feel fine," he said.

"Lie down," ordered Dr. Manson sternly. "We're going to operate and find out what's wrong with you."

"You're not cuttin' into me," said Ollie. He swung his feet to the floor and stood up. "There ain't nothin' wrong with me. I feel wonderful. For the first time in my life I ain't hungry, and I'm spoilin' for trouble. Don't nobody try to stop me."

He started to march across the floor, pushing his way through the protesting doctors.

"This way," said one of the interns near the door. "We'll get your clothes." Ollie looked at her in suspicion, but she went on, "Remember? I'm the one who gave you the tablets to make the pain go away."

"They sure worked," said Ollie happily, and allowed himself to be led along.

He heard the uproar behind him, but he paid no attention. Whatever they wanted, he was getting out of here, fast. There might have been trouble, but at a critical point the public address system swung into operation, thanks to the foresight of his intern friends, who had rigged up a special portable attachment to the microphone. It started calling Dr. Manson, calling Dr. Kolanyi, calling Dr. Pumber, and all the others.

In the confusion, Ollie escaped and found himself, for the first time in his life, a passenger in a taxicab. With him were the two friendly interns, no longer in white.

"Just in case any more of those lumps appear in your stomach," said the female, "you'd better take another couple of tablets."

She was so persuasive that Ollie put up only token resistance. The tablets went down his stomach, and then he settled back to enjoy the cab ride. It was only later that he wondered where they were taking him. By that time, he was too sleepy to wonder very much.

With the aid of the first two tablets, he had digested the equivalent of a tremendous meal. The blood coursed merrily in his veins and arteries, and he had a warm sensation of well-being.

As the taxi sped along, his eyes closed.

"You transmitted the message in one of the latter tablets?" asked Zolto in their native tongue.

"I have explained all that has happened," replied his wife. "They will stop sending food and wait for other directives."

"Good. Now we'll have to get the transfer out of him as soon as possible. We ourselves can operate and he will never be the wiser."

"I wonder," said Pojim. "Once we have the transfer, it will only be a nuisance to us. We'll have to guard it carefully and be in continual fear of losing it. Perhaps it would be more sensible to leave it inside him."

"Inside him? Pojim, my sweet, have you taken leave of your senses?"

"Not at all. It is easier to guard a man than a tiny object. I took a look at one of the X-ray plates, and it is clear that the transfer switch has adhered to his stomach. It will remain there indefinitely. Suppose we focus a transpositor on that stomach of his. Then, as the objects we want arrive from our own universe in their collapsed condition, we can transpose them into our laboratory, enlarge them, and send them off to Aldebaran, where they are needed."

"But suppose that he and that stomach of his move around!"

"He will stay in one place if we treat him well. Don't you see, Zolto? He is a creature who has always lacked food. We shall supply him such food as his own kind have never dreamed of, complete with pandigestion fluid. At the same time, we shall set him to doing light work in order to keep him busy. Much of his task will involve studying and improving himself. And at night we shall receive the things we need from our own universe."

"And when we have enough to supply the colony on Aldebaran II?"

"Then it will be time enough to remove the transfer switch."

Zolto laughed. It was a laugh that would have been curiously out of place in a human being, and if the taxi driver hadn't been so busy steering his way through traffic, he would have turned around to look. Pojim sensed the danger, and held up a warning finger.

Zolto subsided. "You have remarkable ideas, my wife. Still, I see no reason why this should not work. Let us try it."

Ollie awoke to a new life. He was feeling better than he had ever felt in his entire miserable existence. The two interns who had come along with him had been transformed magically into a kindly lady and gentleman, who wished to hire him to do easy work at an excellent salary. Ollie let himself be hired.

He had his choice of things to eat now, but, strangely enough, he no longer had his old hunger. It was as if he were being fed from some hidden source, and he ate, one might almost have said, for the looks of it. The little he did consume, however, seemed to go a long way.

He gained weight, his muscles hardened, his old teeth fell out and new ones appeared. He himself was astonished at this latter phenomenon, but after his previous experience at the hospital, he kept his astonishment to himself. The spots on his lungs disappeared, his spine straightened. After a time he reached a weight of a hundred and ninety pounds, and his eyes were bright and clear. At night he slept the sleep of the just—or the drugged.

At first he was happy. But after several months, there came a feeling of boredom. He sought out Mr. and Mrs. Zolto, and said, "I'm sorry, I can't stay here any longer."

"Why?" asked the lady.

"There's no room here, ma'am, for advancement," he said, almost apologetically. "I've been studyin' and I got ideas about things I can do. All sorts of ideas."

Pojim and Zolto, who had planted the ideas, nodded solemnly.

Pojim said, "We're glad to hear that, Ollie. The fact is that we ourselves had decided to move to—to a warmer climate, some distance away from here. We were wondering how you'd get along without us."

"Don't you worry about me. I'll do fine."

"Well, that's splendid. But it would be convenient to us if you could wait till tomorrow. We'd like to give you something to remember us by."

"I'll be glad to wait, ma'am."

That night Ollie had a strange nightmare. He dreamed that he was on the operating table again, and that the doctors and nurses were once more closing in on him. He opened his mouth to scream, but no sound came out. And then the two interns were there, once more wearing their uniforms.

The female said, "It's all right. It's perfectly all right. We're just removing the transfer switch. In the morning you won't even remember what happened."

And, in fact, in the morning he didn't. He had only a vague feeling that something *had* happened.

They shook hands with him and they gave him a very fine letter of reference, in case he tried to get another job, and Mrs. Zolto presented him with an envelope in which there were several bills whose size later made his eyes almost pop out of his head.

He walked down the street as if it belonged to him, or were going to. Gone was the slouch, gone the bleariness of the eyes, gone the hangdog look.

Gone was all memory of the dismal past.

And then Ollie had a strange feeling. At first it seemed so peculiar that he couldn't figure out what it was. It started in his stomach, which seemed to turn over and almost tie itself into a knot. He felt a twinge of pain and winced almost perceptibly.

It took him several minutes to realize what it was.

For the first time in months, he was hungry.

www.ingramcontent.com/pod-product-compliance
Lightning Source LLC
LaVergne TN
LVHW091238080426
835509LV00009B/1328